HOLLY WEBB

EMILY FEATHER

and the Starlit Staircase

SCHOLASTIC

First published in the UK in 2014 by Scholastic Children's Books
An imprint of Scholastic Ltd
Euston House, 24 Eversholt Street
London, NW1 1DB, UK
Registered office: Westfield Road, Southam, Warwickshire, CV47 0RA
SCHOLASTIC and associated logos are trademarks and/
or registered trademarks of Scholastic Inc.

ISBN 978 1 407 13095 8

A CIP catalogue record for this book
is available from the British Library.

Printed and bound by CPI Group (UK) Ltd, Croydon, CR0 4YY
Papers used by Scholastic Children's Books are made
from wood grown in sustainable forests.

1 3 5 7 9 10 8 6 4 2

This is a work of fiction. Names, characters, places, incidents and
dialogues are products of the author's imagination or are used
fictitiously. Any resemblance to actual people, living or
dead, events or locales is entirely coincidental.

www.scholastic.co.uk

For everyone who has wondered about the end of Emily's story

Emily poked thoughtfully at the sticky, scented mixture for her cake, and closed her eyes.

All her family had told her that her cooking was magical. Lots of people at school said so too, but they didn't mean it in quite the same way. Robin, Emily's younger brother, and her older sisters, Lark and Lory, *knew* that Emily was stirring spells into her cakes and cookies and brownies and fudge.

They understood about magic far better than anyone else could. What they didn't understand was quite where Emily was getting the magic from – it wasn't as if she was a fairy. Not like them.

Emily had found out the truth a couple of months before: that her family weren't her family by blood. She had been adopted. Found. Chosen, her father, Ash, explained. He said it made her even more special. He had found her abandoned on a riverbank and brought her home to be looked after.

Emily added a drop more vanilla extract, and frowned to herself. Being adopted was the simplest part to understand, even though it wasn't easy to know how she should feel. It was the rest of the family set-up that she'd taken a while to get her head around.

All of Emily's family were fairies – and they were important ones. They were close relations of the royal family in a separate faraway world. The house that they lived in was actually a gateway to that other place. It was Ash's job to guard the doors and stop anyone from travelling between the two. Sometimes Emily wondered how she'd got to ten years old without realizing what was going on. Or at least understanding that her family was a bit strange, compared to everyone else's. But she'd grown up with strange, she thought, dipping a teaspoon into her mixture and tasting. For her, strange was normal. She was used to seeing odd things out of the corner of her eye, things that weren't there when she turned round and looked at them properly. She'd never really understood that

3

other people's houses weren't like that.

She'd put her dad's weirdness down to him being an author. Somebody who was always writing about trolls and demons and every kind of monster ought to be a bit different. And her mum was . . . well. Artists were always peculiar, and Eva was an artist, though mostly she drew designs for fabrics.

Emily had always assumed that there was an odd one out in every family, and she was it. The normal one. The boring child, who helpfully made cups of tea and listened when her dad was having a panic over his deadline, or when he had somehow managed to lead half his characters into an exploding volcano with no idea how to get them out again.

Except that now, she wasn't normal any more.

Emily smiled to herself as the cake mixture filled her mouth with sweetness – there was honey, and a soft, cosy buzzing, like bees on lavender. That wasn't normal. That was magic. And it wasn't only good for cooking. Her magic was growing. Last week, she had taken a handful of brownie crumbs and made a tiny, gorgeous cocoa-furred mouse. Robin had begged to keep him as a pet – now he slept in a teacup next to Robin's bed. Emily would never be like Robin, or her sisters, who could fling spells around the house all day. For her, magic was hard – but it was there, and it was beautiful, and special, and so, so exciting.

"Ems! Haven't you finished that yet?" Her older sister Lory was leaning against the kitchen door frame, staring at her impatiently.

"No, I'm still trying to get it right." Emily

frowned. "Why, what's the matter?"

"Dad wants to talk to us. I told him you were cooking, and he got a sort of funny look on his face and said we'd wait till you were finished. So hurry up, will you, please? I want to know what's going on."

Emily wrinkled her nose curiously and sniffed at her cake mixture. It smelled gorgeous, and she was suddenly sure it was ready. She scraped it quickly into the tin, and then, without really thinking what she was doing, she pressed both hands gently against the metal and closed her eyes, just for a second, before she slid the tin into the oven and set the timer.

"What were you doing just then?" Lory asked her, frowning a little.

6

"When? Setting the timer? I always do. Especially because if Dad wants us for something interesting, I might forget to check the cake."

"No, silly! I know what the oven timer is!"

Emily sniffed. "Do you? I've never seen you do more than make toast. And even then you always leave the bread out, and crumbs all over the place." But she was grinning, and Lory only pretended to smack her.

"I meant when you held the tin like that – it almost seemed as though you were talking to it."

"Oh. . ." Emily looked bewildered. "Did I? I don't remember. . ."

Lory nodded, peering at her interestedly, and then at the cake, which was softly glowing in the light of the oven. "You did." She shook her head.

"We should have noticed ages ago what you're doing when you cook. Magic all the way. No wonder you make nicer cakes than anybody else."

Emily eyed the cake too. "Is that what you and Lark meant about magic not being something you do on purpose? Like you don't always have to say spell words? Sometimes it just . . . happens, without you trying to?"

"Mm-hm."

"And it's happening to me too? Just a little bit?" Emily whispered, wanting Lory to tell her about the magic again, to make her sure. She could still taste the cake mixture in her mouth – there was sugar and honey on her tongue, and vanilla in the crack between her front teeth. It tasted very, very good. Imagine being able to make magic

8

without even thinking about it!

Emily hadn't really understood what Robin had meant when he told her that she had magic too. He'd tried to explain that it had leaked into her, from living with them for ten years, and from the house, with its doors to the fairy world. Emily had expected that Lark and Lory and Robin might be able to teach her a few little spells. Easy tricks. But not that magic might grow in her like this. She was beginning to see that maybe it had been growing for a while.

"Oh, Ems. It's been happening for ages, and you just didn't know it." Lory frowned, two pretty lines running down between her perfectly arched eyebrows. "Maybe years, even. We didn't know it either, though. I think that's probably one of the things Dad wants to talk about."

"Is he cross?" Emily looked at Lory worriedly.

Lory shook her head. "I don't think so. A bit worried, maybe. Come on."

Emily peered nervously at their dad as she followed Lory into the tiny writing room under the stairs. But as far as she could see, their father looked quite normal. As normal as he ever did, anyway. He was the least human-looking of her family, even when he was disguised as a human! His skin had an odd, chalky look to it, and he was too much all one colour. Lark and Robin were perched on either arm of his big chair, and Eva was leaning against his desk. And yet the little room under the stairs didn't look cramped, even when Emily sat down on a tower of books and Lory stretched herself out on the rug.

Her father smiled at Emily. "Is the cake done, then?"

"It's in the oven. . ." Emily said uncertainly. She'd hardly spoken to him over the last few days, and she wasn't quite sure what this was all about.

"Don't look at me like that," he murmured, his grey, marble-like eyes darkening a little. "Don't be scared of me, Emily."

She ducked her head, embarrassed and still a little worried. "You're angry with me," she whispered. "For having magic. And for – well, for using it."

"No! I promise, Emily, that's not it." He sighed. "I am angry, furious actually, but not with you. We were stupid, that's why I'm angry. We should have realized how much living here would change you.

11

And we've been too – too strict, I suppose. With you all."

Emily saw Robin and Lark and Lory shift, leaning closer, their eyes brightening. Robin's eyes definitely got bigger. So this wasn't just another lecture on being careful, and keeping their secrets, and never showing any magic, and, and, and. . .

Eva shook her head, her beautiful dark red hair curling and twisting around her shoulders. It was glittering fiercely, the way it did when she got angry. Little fiery sparks fizzled into the air, and Emily eyed her mother worriedly. But Eva didn't shout. She looked tired. Almost defeated, as though she had lost a battle. Her eyes were red, and Emily wondered if she might have been crying. "I still don't think this is right," she said sadly. "So dangerous. . ."

Dangerous... Something fluttered at the corners of Emily's mind, something soft and golden-feathered and eager. But she brushed it away. It was just another stray wisp of spell. Magic was swirling in the air of the tiny room now, and excitement was building.

Gruff, Eva's huge black dog, suddenly arrived in the doorway, and the hair along his spine was standing up. He padded silently to Eva and sat down next to her, so still he could have been carved from ebony. She laid her hand on his massive neck and leaned on him just a little. Emily could see the faint relief in her mother's eyes. Whatever was happening, Eva was unhappy about it, and Gruff was helping her to be strong.

Their father sighed. "You're too worried about

13

them all, Eva! I know you just want to keep them safe. I understand – particularly now. . . But they're too old to be babied."

Why now? Emily wondered, but there was no time to ask, and she was as eager as the others to hear what their father was going to say.

"We've always said no magic outside the house, and that you should only be doing the slightest charms and glamours anyway. But. . ."

All four of the children stared at him eagerly.

"Well – it isn't working, is it? We thought by banning magic we'd be keeping you safe, but all we've done is make you hide your spells from us. If you'd trusted us to help you, you wouldn't have needed to go chasing off into the fairy world."

Emily flushed, and stared at the faded rug

beneath her feet. It had seemed at the time as though there was nothing else they could do. But perhaps he was right. She had never been meant to go to the fairy world. Humans didn't; it was too dangerous. But she couldn't help it! The first time had been an accident. Emily had only just found out that she was adopted, and that her family were not her family. That they weren't even human. She was so confused and angry that all she wanted to do was get away, and somehow she had broken through into that other world. She had woken up to find herself surrounded by fairies – beautiful but dangerous, and hungry for the strength and life a human child could bring them. They had charmed Emily, begging her to stay, and of course she hadn't understood what they were doing. She had only seen their loveliness, and the gentle way they spoke. Lady Anstis, their leader, had made Emily feel so welcome. So wanted. She had only just escaped, rescued by Lark and Lory, with the help of a water-sprite girl.

But then Emily had gone back again, on purpose, to rescue a friend. Sasha, that same water sprite, was being hunted because she had helped them. And the rescue had worked – now Sasha was living in the garden pond. In fact, Emily was pretty sure she liked it there. The pond seemed to be magically bigger, and there were frogs lurking under all the bushes in the garden, and jewelled dragonflies dive-bombing the grass.

The last time Emily had been to the fairy world, she had gone to the rescue again, this time with

Lark and Robin, and Sasha too. Lory had been stolen away by a fairy, who'd bewitched her with a song. Even Lark and Lory hadn't known what he was – they'd thought he was just an annoying boy from school – until the spell had begun to work and Lory had brought him into the house. The house had been what Dantis was after all along – a way back to the fairy world he'd been exiled from for so long. He hated the human world, and he'd been desperate to return, desperate enough not to care who he hurt on the way. Dantis had enchanted Lory so deeply that she'd threatened to hurt Lark, her own twin, if anyone told their parents what he was doing. They'd had to rescue Lory by themselves.

Emily glanced at the white cat that was draped

along the back of her father's armchair. The treacherous Dantis was much better as a cat. Right now he was eyeing Gruff cautiously, and flexing his claws in and out of the velvet covering of the chair.

"So now we can do any spells we like?" Robin asked, his voice high and squeaky with excitement.

Eva looked at him sharply. "Provided you're not hurting anyone. . ."

Robin widened his eyes angelically and shook his head.

Eva sighed and reached out to stroke his hair, twisting one of the dark red curls around her finger for a moment, until Robin rolled his eyes and pulled away. He hated being fussed at.

"And no blowing anything up," Ash added, in a suspicious voice. "Just – just be sensible, all right?"

18

He sighed. "And still no magic outside the house."

"Awww, Dad!" Lark put on a pleading face. "None? Just a few little bits at school? Come on. . ."

"Too dangerous."

"We wouldn't get caught," Lory added pleadingly. But Emily could tell that neither of her sisters thought begging was going to work. And they didn't mind all that much. Being allowed to use any magic they liked within the house was far more than any of them had expected.

"What about Emily?" Robin asked suddenly. "Is she allowed to do any magic she likes too?"

Ash nodded, frowning a little. "Yee-eees. Except you need to be extra careful, Emily. Your magic's different. Something new, and we don't know much about it yet."

"But we're here, Emily," Eva added anxiously. "Ask us and we can help, even if we're all feeling our way with your magic."

"And there's always your water sprite to help," Ash added, his voice dropping a little, and Emily gave a tiny sigh. He was still cross about her bringing Sasha back. No one was supposed to make the journey between the worlds without permission, even if was life or death, as it had been for Sasha.

Then her father smiled, showing his surprisingly white teeth. "Please can you bring me a bit of cake when it's done?"

Emily nodded. If magic was allowed now, she was going to have to go and think very carefully about what to put in the icing. . .

"What is it?" Lory prodded disdainfully at the greyish slice of cake in front of her, and Emily sighed.

"I don't really know. You all say I put magic in my cooking, but I've never actually tried to before... It always just happened without me doing anything. So this time I..." Emily poked at the solid lump of cake. "Well, I sort of *tried* to make a magic cake. After Dad said yesterday that any spells were allowed, I put magic in it on purpose. But it didn't work right."

Lory nodded. "I guessed. What was it supposed to do?"

"Stop Robin being hungry. It was meant to be super-filling. So there was some left for the rest of us."

Lory giggled, and suddenly Emily saw how much of her sister's magic had been buried inside her. Now that they didn't have to hide, Lory's pure happiness spilled out of her with the laughter, and a small golden bird popped into the air above her head, fluttering and swooping round the kitchen. It darted over the plate of cake and seized a crumb in its beak. Lory put a hand over her mouth, practically choking with laughter as the bird stopped mid-air, its wings buzzing with sudden panicked effort. It lurched heavily out of the kitchen window in a series of clumsy swoops and flaps, and disappeared into the ivy growing up the outside wall. Confused twittering floated back to them.

"Well, it worked, didn't it? He's not going to be hungry for that, Ems, and there'll be plenty left."

"Don't be so mean," Emily muttered crossly. "I really tried. I don't know why it didn't work. It was supposed to be delicious and squidgy and banana-toffee flavoured."

"Maybe you tried too hard," Lory said thoughtfully. "Cakes are light, aren't they, unless it's that fab chocolate-fudge brick thing you do. Too much trying might make a magic cake – um, like this. . ."

"Mmmm. I suppose so." Emily sighed. "Perhaps it's better just to let the magic happen naturally. But that's no good when you're really trying to do something in particular. Like – learn my spellings. I can't just naturally let that happen. It won't. And Mrs Daunt's given us loads, it's not fair. I hate the way we get them on Fridays – it ruins the whole weekend."

Lory sighed and rolled her eyes, but having her the freedom to use her magic all the time seemed to have made her a lot less grumpy too. Emily could hardly remember the last time she'd sat and chatted like this. Like sisters in books did. It helped that Lark was buried in her room doing something super-secret. And of course, Lory's boyfriend had turned out to be a slimeball fairy

24

exile, who wanted to murder the fairy king for revenge. And then he'd been turned into a cat.

Lory was bored, and Emily was company.

"Get the list." Glittering sparks shot between Lory's fingers as she snapped them, and Emily darted into the hallway and pulled her spelling sheet out of her bag. Perhaps Lory could just beam them into her brain somehow. She held out the piece of paper and stared at her sister hopefully.

"Can you really not spell the months of the year?" Lory raised her eyebrows, and Emily's shoulders slumped.

"No," she admitted. "You know I'm awful at spelling. And they don't look how they sound."

"Maybe." Lory eyed her, a little puzzled frown pinching her nose. It was a look Emily was used

25

to. Lark and Lory and Robin all seemed to be naturally clever, even though Robin always got into trouble for not listening, and wriggling about too much. They just didn't understand how someone could not be able to spell. And Emily didn't understand how someone *could*.

"What about if we. . . No, that won't work. . ." Lory sniffed. "Hey, have you still got those icing pens?"

"Yes," Emily said doubtfully, turning to get the box down from one of the cupboards.

"And get me a biscuit!" Lory was enjoying herself now, Emily could tell. It made her nervous. She handed Lory a packet of chocolate digestives, which she'd hidden behind the flour.

Her sister pulled two out of the packet and

munched on one of them thoughtfully as she squeezed the icing pens between her long fingers.

"Yellow," she said at last, handing the others to Emily to put away. "Definitely the best colour. Pink is sickly, the green sets my teeth on edge and blue food just looks wrong."

"All right," Emily said meekly. She quite liked the pink icing herself, but if Lory was going to teach her how to spell, she didn't care what colour they used.

"Hold the tube," Lory snapped. "With me, there. No, tighter!" She wrapped Emily's fingers round the tiny tube, with her own long delicate fingers over them, and together they started to write on the top of the chocolate digestive.

"Think about tracing the words out in sugar,"

27

Lory murmured as the icing spiralled out from the centre of the biscuit. Emily had been sure they wouldn't fit all twelve months on one digestive, but Lory wrote with the icing as if it were any other pen, her script twirly, with little flourishes on the Ys.

"Remember the sweetness. . ." Lory's voice was sweet too, and a sugary haze seemed to float around them as the magic built. Emily could taste caramel in the air.

"Now what do we do?" Emily whispered as Lory wrote December, and added a border of fancy stars around the edge of the biscuit.

"You eat it, of course!"

Emily eyed her suspiciously. "It's not going to turn into something horrible?"

Lory pretended to look hurt. "Of course not."

"All right. . . Do I have to eat all of it?"

"Yes! Or you'll only be able to spell half the words!"

Emily picked the biscuit up. She could feel the magic in it, buzzing against the skin of her fingertips, and the scent was delicious: sweet, but not sickly. She hoped this worked, that it wasn't just some silly game of Lory's. She nibbled the edge of the biscuit, and the sweetness rolled on to her tongue. Somehow, along with it came a sense of the words, dancing just out of her reach, and she took another big bite. Her spelling words started to march across the front of her mind in strong, sugary letters, and she quickly gobbled the rest of the biscuit.

Lory looked at her expectantly. "So, did it work? Spell August."

Emily swallowed the last few crumbs, licked

icing off her teeth, and smiled blissfully. She knew it. She knew she knew it. It was the nicest feeling. "A – u – g – u – s – t."

"There." Lory nodded, pleased. "Easy. You'll always know them now."

Emily hugged her. "Thanks, Lory! You know, it's funny, but now when I think about the words, I can taste them too. . . June tastes like strawberries."

"Does February taste like some sort of disgusting stew?" Lory shivered. She hated cold weather.

"Ummm. More like cough sweets, I think. And it's still a really hard one to spell. Maybe that's why it doesn't taste so nice." She sighed happily, slipping into a chair next to Lory and resting her chin on her hands. They sat there together, thoughtful and sugar-dreamy, until Emily murmured, "What did Mum and Dad mean, yesterday, about Mum being worried and wanting to keep us all safe?"

"She always does." Lory yawned. "You know what she's like. She fusses about stuff."

"Yes, but he said *particularly now*. What was that about?"

"Did he?" Lory sat up straighter, frowning. "I don't know... Have you noticed anything different? About Mum?"

Emily gazed at her big sister, her eyes worried. "What sort of thing?"

"She just seems odd." Lory picked up the icing tube again and kneaded it between her fingers.

"She was crying," Lark said behind them, and Emily jumped.

"How long have you been standing there?"

"Not long." Lark twisted one of Emily's dark curly bunches round her finger and sat down next to her. "But you're right. I think there is something funny going on."

"Actually crying?" Lory asked, frowning, and Emily looked round worriedly at Lark. She'd hardly ever seen her mother cry. But the last couple of times she'd curled up on the old sofa in her mum's studio, borrowing a sketch pad and a handful of pastels, Eva had been very quiet. Not unhappy, though, Emily was almost sure.

"Maybe it wasn't *bad* crying. . ." she said, hoping that Lark and Lory would know what she meant.

"Maybe. But she's definitely all emotional at the moment. She keeps hugging Robin," Lark pointed out. "He's getting really antsy about it."

It was true – Robin wriggled and growled and made faces, but Eva did keep on cuddling him. And she'd been fussing at Emily too, dropping kisses on her hair as she went past, patting her face. Eva had always been a person who hugged, but Lark was right, she was a lot more cuddly just now.

"Why is she doing it?" Emily murmured anxiously. She thought back to the beginning of the summer, when she'd been worrying about her whole family acting strange. She'd wondered at the time if her parents were splitting up. Her best friend Rachel's mum and dad were divorced, and the weird atmosphere in the house had felt a lot like what Rachel described before her parents had split.

"She's – she's not fighting with Dad, is she?" But almost as soon as she said it, Emily shook her head, and Lark and Lory snorted disbelievingly. Their parents were far too happy, even if they had argued about letting Emily and the others use their magic more.

"No." Lark shook her head firmly. "But something's happening. I hate secrets. Unless I'm the one keeping them, of course," she added, her voice annoyingly smug. A faint pink haze swirled around her just for a moment. Pink was obviously a smug colour. Lark's dress was definitely pinker than it had been when she'd changed after school. As Emily watched, tiny glittering sequins sewed themselves all round the hem, and Lark chuckled to herself and twirled, so that the sequins sparkled and danced.

"What have you been doing up there in your

34

room?" Lory begged. "You have to tell me, I'm your sister. Your twin sister," she added, glancing at Emily.

"Nope." Lark smirked. "It's special, and I'm enjoying myself. I'm not telling anyone, not till it's ready. Anyway." She flicked her fingers, wisping her sisters' minds away from thoughts about her room. Emily saw delicate amber-coloured stars floating towards her over the table, and she felt suddenly desperate for a cup of tea. She found herself standing up and reaching for a mug from the wooden dresser.

But then Lory gently touched her arm, and the amber haze flickered and faded away. "It's a spell, Emily. Don't."

She didn't even like tea!

Emily dropped the mug back down on the shelf

35

with a bang and scowled at Lark. "Don't do that! You can just say you don't want to tell us, you don't have to put spells on me. And tea's horrible!"

"Stop trying to glamour us, Lark." Lory rolled her eyes. "You're useless at it. And we're going to find out, you know."

Lark shrugged. "Sure you are, when I let you. Anyway, what I was going to say, before you so rudely interrupted, was that I think we should ask Mum and Dad what's going on. At dinner."

Emily swallowed nervously, and nodded. It might feel too much like the evening when her family had told her who they really were. But she hated secrets too. She wanted to know. Besides, it wasn't as if they could tell her they were fairies all over again – and nothing could be as shocking as that.

"You ask," Lory breathed, catching Emily's eye as she slid into her chair. Dinner seemed to be one of Eva's interesting creations with mushrooms. Eva liked mushrooms a lot, which did make sense. Fairies were always sitting on toadstools in books. But they'd been having mushrooms ever so often recently, and Emily was getting a bit bored with them. Perhaps she should offer to cook dinner sometimes, instead of just making puddings. . .

"Emily!" Lory hissed.

"Why me?" Emily glared at her.

"Spellings!"

"Oh, all right. . ."

"What are you two whispering about?" Eva smiled at them dreamily, and Emily swallowed.

There were golden feathery wisps around her again; she could almost the feel the feathers stroking at her cheek. Someone laughed, almost too far away for Emily to hear, and she glanced around the kitchen, confused for a second. It was as if someone had been trying to talk to her.

"Go on!" Lory whispered, and the tiny feathers floated away as Emily blinked. Then she scooted sideways on her chair, before her big sister could elbow her in the ribs. Lory looked rather surprised, and Emily smirked at her. Her magic was definitely getting stronger.

"We were wondering if anything special is happening," she said in a rush, leaning across the table to look at her mother.

Eva's eyes widened and sharpened suddenly,

her dreamy look disappearing like clouds blown away in the wind. The soft, dark grey of her eyes was suddenly shot through with bluish glints. It was as if she'd woken up inside, and Emily shifted back a little, staring at her nervously.

"What sort of something special?" their father asked. His voice was gentle and quiet, but it made Emily feel like talking. The words wanted to spill out of her in a river.

"It's very rude to do that," she told him quickly, and then she gritted her teeth, determined to hold the words back. His spell was lining up all their questions and suspicions inside her head, ready to march out. "You shouldn't use magic to make people do things!" she finished in a rush.

Ash blinked, his eyelids slowly hooding over

his milky grey eyes, and smiled apologetically at Emily. "Sorry. I actually didn't mean to. . . Yes, it was rude."

The spell faded away, and Emily felt the words melt back into her mind. "I was going to tell you anyway," she said, a little coldly. "We thought something might be happening, that's all. Mum's . . . different." She looked sideways at Eva, who blinked.

"Too grabby," Robin muttered, eyeing his mother irritably. "You keep mauling me about and kissing me. You know I hate it."

"And Dad said that you were worried about keeping us safe," Emily explained. "*Particularly now*, he said. What's happening now? That's what we wanted to know." She stopped suddenly, glancing between them with anxious eyes.

However much Lark and Lory had laughed when she worried about their parents splitting up, Emily couldn't dismiss it from her mind entirely. She had spent so long comforting Rachel – and Rachel's mum and dad had always looked perfectly happy to her. The thought of something like that happening to her own family terrified her.

"Emily, what are you frightened of?" her mother asked. Her eyes had softened to grey again, and they were clouded over with tears.

"You *are* crying!" Lark said sharply. "There is something wrong."

"Nothing's wrong," Eva protested, sniffing and shaking her head, but jewelled tears were glittering around her eyes. "But we should tell them," she added, brushing the sparkling drops away with the back of her hand and glancing at Ash.

"Mmmm." He nodded, but he didn't say anything. He looked a little nervous, Emily thought, and her heart began to thud again, swelling with every thumping beat, so that it blocked her throat and made it seem hard to swallow.

"Tell us what?" Robin demanded. "Stop making us wait."

Eva took a deep breath, and Emily felt Robin's hand slip into hers under the table. She squeezed it gratefully and stared at her mother.

Eva smiled at them, but her eyes were still wet and her voice trembled a little. "I'm going to have a baby."

Emily squeaked with pain as Robin's nails dug into her palm.

42

"Sorry. . ." he muttered. "A baby?"

"Yes. In a month or so."

Emily stared at her mother, and leaned sideways a bit to look at her middle. From the corner of her eye she could see Lark and Lory doing the same thing. "You haven't got a bump."

"It's a glamour," Lory said flatly. "I can see it, now that I look. So, when were you going to tell us? When it arrived? 'Hello, darlings, this is your new brother or sister'?"

Her mother swallowed, ducking her head. "I wanted to tell you months ago," she murmured. "But so much has been happening. I didn't want to break the news when we'd only just told Emily the truth about us all. It seemed too much. . . We all needed time to settle down again together. And then Dantis." She glanced up at the white cat, who was sprawled elegantly across the top of the wooden dresser, his green eyes glinting curiously. "I've wanted to tell you, so much. I wanted you to be excited."

"Is it a boy or a girl?" Robin asked strangely.

"I don't know." Eva smiled at him gratefully. "I could tell, if I wanted to, but I was leaving it as a surprise."

"Well, that worked," Lory said under her breath. "I'm definitely surprised."

Gruff's head appeared over the edge of the table, and for once, he wasn't sniffing for food. He stared narrowly at Lory, his muzzle wrinkling and a low growl escaping from his mouth.

"How could you not tell us?" Lark asked. She

44

looked as though she was about to cry too. "No wonder we thought you were being weird. A baby. . ."

"It's not having my room," Lory said suddenly.

"No one has asked you to give up your room!" Ash glared at her. "Lory, you sound like a five-year-old. Bad-tempered and sulky."

"Well, you're *treating* us like five-year-olds!" Lory yelled, pushing her chair back. "Did you really think it would be OK? You've known about this for months and not said anything to us! What else are you hiding?"

Emily shivered, watching Lory's hair lifting around her face, puffing out into a cloud of streaked blonde as her anger shimmered through it. Lory scared her when she was angry – and the worst thing was, she'd inherited the snarly temper from Ash. Across the table, he was reacting in just the same way. A haze of almost-visible fury was rising off him as he listened to Lory shouting. Gruff pressed himself close against Eva, and his growl grew louder, until it exploded into furious barking. Emily shuddered and jammed the back of her hand against her mouth to keep from whimpering. Gruff's bark seemed to tear at something inside her. It swirled with Lory's shouts and her father's furious intake of breath to build a tension that Emily could actually see, thickening around them in a purplish storm cloud. It made Emily feel sick.

But even so, for once, Emily was glad that Lory was kicking off. Lory was saying everything that

Emily wanted to say – and if Emily had tried to say it, she would have cried. She knew she would. The tears were at the back of her nose already. It was a lot easier to let Lory say it for her.

It wasn't that she didn't like the idea of a baby brother or sister. But her mother looked so happy – or she had, until Lory had started shouting. Eva had one hand resting on her tummy even now, as if she were trying to protect the child inside her from the angry voices. This little fairy child, who would really be hers, like Lory and Lark and Robin were.

And like Emily wasn't.

Even with her little bit of magic, the magic that she had been so happy about, Emily would never be one of them. She would never really belong.

3

"Where will the baby sleep?" Emily asked her mother the next morning as she watched her nibble a piece of toast. Lark and Lory had gone out – Lory was still being sulky, and she had a way of stamping around and slamming doors that made the whole house feel fragile. It was definitely easier to breathe without her around.

Eva looked at her a little cautiously. As though

she was expecting Emily to be as bad-tempered as Lory had been. "Well . . . at first in our room. In a Moses basket. And then, probably in that little room just next to the bathroom."

Emily blinked at her, trying to think where she meant. There *wasn't* a room next to the bathroom, little or otherwise. "Mum, that's a cupboard. With all the towels in?"

Her mum smiled at her. "I know. But . . . well, it needn't stay that way."

"What, you can make it bigger?" Emily looked round their massive kitchen, suddenly wondering if it had always been this size. Did her mum just squash another cupboard in whenever she was having difficulty putting the washing-up away?

"I can make it feel bigger. It won't actually be

49

bigger," Eva explained. "But it'll be big enough for a little one. . ." She bit her lip and looked at Emily anxiously. As though she was worried about what Emily would say next. But Eva was always so calm, so unflappable. *What if the baby changes everything?* Emily wondered miserably. Her mother was obviously thinking about it all the time. It was stupid and selfish to worry that her parents wouldn't love her any more, when they had a new baby. Emily knew she was being silly.

It didn't mean she could stop herself thinking it, though.

"I wonder who the baby will look like," she murmured, glancing at her mum's bump. She had let the glamour fade away now, and she was obviously pregnant. So pregnant that it was hard to see how they hadn't noticed. Emily could almost make out the outline of the tiny person under Eva's flowered tunic. As she watched, the imprint of a tiny hand appeared – as though it were reaching out to her. Emily blinked and shook her head. Of course it hadn't. She knew that sometimes you could see babies kick, or feel them. But you couldn't see a hand, a little hand with the fingers outstretched in a baby wave. That was *stupid*.

Eva ran her own hand over the bump lovingly, and smiled. She was even sitting differently, eased forward in her chair.

It just showed how much glamours could hide, Emily thought, shivering.

Her mum gave her another worried look. She'd seen the shiver, Emily realized, staring down at the woodgrain pattern on the table so as not to meet Eva's eyes.

"It won't look like me," she whispered.

"Oh, Emily. . ." Her mum's voice shook. "It'll be your brother or sister too. Please don't think like that. You know we all belong together." She reached out her hand to Emily, but Emily shoved her chair back so Eva couldn't reach her. She couldn't bear to be told that it was all right, that she was imagining things again. . .

"I don't want to talk about it!" Emily said quickly, jumping up. "I'm sorry! I just can't!"

She plunged away out of the room, practically knocking Robin over in the doorway.

"Oi!" he growled, but then as she dashed up the stairs, Emily heard his footsteps behind her.

She turned back on the landing just before she stepped on to the stairs up to her room, folded her arms, and glared at him.

"Why are you following me?"

Robin shrugged, looking a bit embarrassed. "Wanted to see if you were OK, that's all. You looked upset. . . And Mum went off to her studio. Is it the – you know?" He hunched up one shoulder in an awkward shrug, as if he knew that Emily didn't want to talk about it. "The baby?"

"Mmmm." Emily jumped up a couple of the steep steps, and then sat down. She loved her stairs. They were crooked, and usually a bit dusty, but there was something friendly about them. They were good for sitting and thinking.

"Do you mind? About the baby?" she asked

Robin curiously. He was the youngest, and Lark and Lory always claimed he was spoiled. Especially because he was a boy. Emily didn't think he actually was spoiled – it was just that he was good at getting away with stuff, because he simply slipped away when someone was about to tell him off. And whatever he did wrong, Lark and Lory or Emily had probably done it before him, so their parents simply weren't very shocked.

Robin sat down sideways a few steps up, leaning against the wall and hugging his knees. "I don't think I mind," he said slowly. "I mean — babies are really noisy, I suppose. . . And messy. There's going to be baby stuff all over the place. And Mum's already getting a bit, um, airy-fairy. . ." Robin sniggered at his own joke. "That's just going

54

to get worse." He brightened. "Which might not be a bad thing. I can't see her fussing over whether I've done my homework or not. *And* I won't be the youngest any more. I'll have somebody to boss around now." He grinned, his eyes sparkling even in the dim light of the staircase. "I think it might be fun."

Then he looked up at Emily. "You're not happy about it, are you? Don't you like babies?"

Emily shrugged. "They're cute – I mean, I've cuddled people at school's little brothers and sisters. But I don't go all gooey about them. Not like Rachel; she's always been desperate for a baby sister." She sighed and met Robin's eerily green eyes. She was sure he could see some of what she was thinking. "It isn't the actual baby," she admitted miserably, scuffing at the step with her plimsoll. "It's just that the baby's really going to belong. It'll be special. Like you all are."

Robin leaned his head back and bumped it against the wall frustratedly. "Not this again, Emily! I've told you loads of times none of us think like that about you."

"Sorry . . . I know you have. And I do believe you. . . I can't help it, though. A baby just makes me feel even more that I'm different. I suppose I'm jealous," she said, feeling her cheeks burn scarlet.

"You and Lory together," Robin muttered. "I don't know why *she's* making such a fuss." Then he looked up at Emily again, his eyes suddenly hard, like green glass. "Do you wish you lived with

56

your own family? Is that why you go on about not belonging?"

"No!" Emily gasped. "I love you, you know I do. And they abandoned me." She sighed shakily. "I wonder sometimes, that's all. I wish I knew what it was like. What happened. Why they – didn't want me." She swallowed hard. "Look, Robin . . . just go away? Please? I don't want to talk about it."

"These stairs don't belong to you, you know," Robin growled crossly. "Just because they only go up to your room. I can sit on them if I want." But he got up and stomped heavily down the stairs, each step leaving a little puff of glittering dust.

Emily watched him go, and then she stood up. She needed – she wasn't quite sure what. Time out. Time *away*. No fairies, no magic, no family. She shivered again as the nasty little voice at the back of her mind whispered, *You've already got no family. . .*

Emily flung herself down the stairs, running headlong into the kitchen and grabbing the phone from the window sill. She stabbed out Rachel's number with trembling fingers, hoping her best friend would answer.

"Rachel?"

"Are you all right, Emily?" Rachel sounded worried, and Emily caught her breath, trying to stop herself sounding so shaky.

"Yeah. Sorry. It's just . . . I had a fight with my mum. There's some stuff going on. . . Weird family stuff, I'll tell you when I see you. Look, Rach, can I come for a sleepover? Do you think your mum would let me?"

58

Rachel snorted with laughter. "Of course she would. She loves you, Emily. Do you want to come now?" she asked hopefully. "I was supposed to be going shopping with Mum, but someone from work called again." Rachel was an only child, and she spent her time shuttling between her mum's flat and her dad's. She had lovely rooms in both, and loads of nice stuff – her dad had bought her a mobile phone, which Emily really envied. But both her parents worked full-time, and Emily knew Rachel got lonely sometimes. Her mum was probably catching up on work.

"Yes. Yes, please. I'll explain what's going on then, OK? I've just got to leave a note for my mum."

Emily hurried back upstairs and threw her

pyjamas and toothbrush into a rucksack, and grabbed her sleeping bag. She scribbled a quick note – *Gone to Rachel's for sleepover* – and left it on the kitchen table. Then she slipped along the hallway, darting past the passage that led to her mum's workroom and fumbling with the lock on the front door. Her dad would know that someone had opened it. He had spell-guards on all the doors, but they were more about keeping an eye on who came in than anyone trying to sneak out. He probably wouldn't even notice that she had gone.

Emily closed the door behind her, and the brass mermaid door knocker shifted a little, chiming against the panels of the door with a sweet, bright note. Emily looked up at it in surprise, and the mermaid stared back. She was softened and worn by years of hands, but now her blurred features had sharpened to life again, and she looked suspicious. Her tail twitched and slapped against the door, and there was a faraway whiff of salt and dry seaweed.

"What?" Emily muttered, taking a step further away.

"Where are you going, Emily Feather?" the mermaid demanded.

Emily hadn't actually expected her to answer – the mermaid had never spoken to her before, although Emily had seen her move – and she gulped and said nothing.

"Are you surprised to hear me talk?" She gave Emily a teasing smile and added, "Didn't you know that I could?"

Another thing she hadn't known. Emily shook her head and turned to go.

"Ah, don't run off! Please! Come back here, Emily," she coaxed. "This isn't right. . ."

"What do you know?" Emily whispered, looking back unwillingly. "It's nothing to do with you."

"I'm part of the house." The mermaid wriggled and stiffly reached out one burnished arm, the sun glinting on the brass so it glowed buttery. "Don't go." Her voice creaked a little too, and Emily wondered when she'd spoken last. "You mustn't run. . ."

"Because you'll get into trouble?" Emily suggested, rather bitterly, but the mermaid looked surprised – or Emily thought she did. It was hard to tell with her being made of metal.

62

"Of course not. Because you belong here."

"I go out all the time!"

"Not like this." The mermaid shook her head, and her stiff metal hair jangled. "You're pulling away. Leaving." She shuddered, and a shadow ran over the gleaming metal. "And there's a strong wind to take you far away, Emily Feather. Don't go."

"I have to," Emily whispered, and the metal girl shook her hair again, her eyes beginning to glow, as if she was waking up more fully. Perhaps the mermaid was going to try and stop her, Emily thought, taking another anxious step back. She pressed her hands over her ears and turned away, racing as fast as she could down the path, her bag banging against her side.

"Beware!" the mermaid cried sharply. "You

63

belong here, Emily Feather. Remember that! Come back!"

But Emily was already gone, and the mermaid's voice was lost in the wind as she whispered again, "Come back. . . Please. . ."

Emily didn't stop running until she was a good way along the road, halfway between her house and Rachel's. There it felt as if she was far enough away to stop any spell pulling her back.

"Are you all right?" Rachel demanded when Emily turned up at the door of the flat, red in the face and gasping. "Were you running? What for?"

"I just wanted to," Emily wheezed. "Felt like it. Can I come in?"

"You are funny sometimes," Rachel told her as Emily followed her through the pristine flat to her bedroom. "Mum's fine about the sleepover. I said your mum was OK with it, though." Rachel looked back and eyed Emily thoughtfully. "Does she even know?"

"I left a note," Emily muttered, squishing herself into Rachel's furry beanbag. "She *will* know."

"So you just walked out?" Rachel looked shocked, and Emily shrugged. Rachel didn't know anything about Emily's family or the magic, but Emily had told her that she was adopted.

"There's stuff going on, like I said. Mum told us, last night. She's having a baby."

"A baby!" Rachel squeaked joyfully, and Emily couldn't help thinking how pleased Eva would have been if she and Lark and Lory had reacted like that the night before. "When?"

"Oh. . ." Emily blinked. They hadn't actually asked, but she had a feeling that fairy babies didn't stick to firm schedules the way human ones did – or were meant to. "Quite soon, I think. . ."

"I hadn't noticed her getting bigger," Rachel said curiously. Then she nodded. "But actually, your mum always wears those lovely drapey sort of dresses. I probably wouldn't have noticed. That's so exciting. . ." Then she trailed off as she finally saw the distinctly unexcited look on Emily's face. "Isn't it?"

"I know it should be," Emily explained, sinking further into the beanbag and staring at the ceiling. "But it isn't. I'm not just being jealous!" she added, struggling up on her elbows to try and look at Rachel. "It probably sounds like it, but I'm

66

not. Don't you see? The baby properly belongs. I don't."

Rachel was silent, and Emily held herself up uncomfortably on the squidgy fur, waiting for her friend to say something.

"Sorry," Rachel murmured at last. "I'd forgotten."

"Really?" Emily pulled herself into a sitting position again and stared at her. Not being truly part of her family was such a big thing – how could Rachel have forgotten about it?

"Mmm. You always seem like you belong. Especially you and Robin – I mean, you're just like anyone with an annoying little brother, Emily. But I suppose a new baby would make it weird. Just because it's different to how you came to be part of the family."

67

Emily sighed. "Exactly. But I don't want to think about it any more. Have you got any ice cream? Do you think we could just do normal stuff? Watch DVDs, and maybe make random mixtures out of all the bottles in the bathroom? The stuff we always do. And eat ice cream. . ."

Rachel knelt in front of the beanbag and gave her a hug. "It's OK. We've got lots of ice cream. And marshmallows. And a bottle of that squirty chocolate sauce."

Emily lay curled up in her sleeping bag, listening to Rachel's soft, unworried breathing. It had been a good idea to come. She had needed to get out of the house – to breathe some air that wasn't laden with spells. Her family were so powerful, so bewitching, that with them around her it was sometimes hard to think for herself. Rachel's flat, and Rachel's everydayness, and Rachel's nice, normal mum, made Emily feel as if her own house was a strange sort of dream.

It was a dream she loved, though. However much she moaned about Lark and Lory bossing her around, and Robin teasing her, and her mum fussing about. Eva had called earlier on, Rachel's mum had said, wanting to check that Emily had remembered her sleeping bag. It was just an excuse. She'd wanted to check that Emily was all right, and she'd actually made it to Rachel's. Emily was glad that her mum hadn't marched round and told Rachel's mum she hadn't really said she could stay over.

Emily sat up, wrapping her arms around her knees, and gazed into the darkness. She hoped her mum was all right. Maybe she was awake too, worrying. Emily almost hoped that she was – not because she wanted her mum to be unhappy (although it would be nice to be missed). But if her mum was unhappy, then at least it meant she cared.

When she'd marched out that morning, Emily had been angry and miserable. She'd been thinking that she'd never belong, so why should she go back?

But of course the answer was, because she wanted to. Because she loved them.

If only she could be sure that they loved her.

4

It didn't seem to Emily as though she fell asleep. She didn't remember being sleepy at all. She went from lying there in the dark, with Rachel fast asleep beside her and making her feel all the more lonely in her wakefulness, to dreaming. It was one of those dreams where she knew she was dreaming – she had that strange sense of being broken away from the real world.

But so often over the last few weeks, dreams had been more than dreams. She had travelled to the fairy world, sometimes without even meaning to. Fairy people had been reaching out to her through her dreaming too, for years. She hadn't known what was happening when she was little, but now she was almost sure that some of her strangest dreams had been real.

Emily was sitting on Rachel's window sill. It was cold, because the window was wide open, but she couldn't quite feel it, so it was all right. She could see herself, still asleep, huddled up in her sleeping bag. But part of her, perhaps the most important part, was gazing out into the darkness, watching the stars. The orange glow of the street lamps had faded, and the stars seemed so much bigger, and clearer, as though they were reaching down to her. Emily blinked slowly as a shooting star burned across the midnight velvet of the sky towards her. She was awake enough in her dreamworld to wonder when it would stop, and then to think, a little anxiously, that it *wasn't* stopping.

And then she saw that it wasn't a star at all.

Shimmering in a silver-white dress, Lady Anstis stepped towards her out of the air and stood before the window. She wasn't floating – she wasn't actually there, Emily decided. She was still in the fairy world, and she was standing in a doorway. *She must be very powerful*, Emily mused dreamily, *to have opened a door in the sky. I wonder how she's done it? Is it because I'm here? I suppose*

I'm a link between here and there. And she knows me. I'm helping her open this door. . .

"Of course you are, Emily darling," Anstis whispered. "You're so strong, you see? And so clever. Such a clever girl."

"I'm really not."

"Oh, but you are! It makes me so angry, Emily, catching wisps of your thoughts. You say that Lark and Lory and Robin are the special ones, and you think you're nothing. But you have it completely the wrong way round!"

"I'm not a fairy, though." Emily frowned at her, but secretly she was wishing Anstis would go on. Her voice was so soft and silky, and her words seemed to wrap Emily up. She felt warmer already.

"Exactly," Anstis whispered. "You're not a

fairy, but look what you can do. I saw that little chocolate mouse, Emily dearest, I saw him in your dreams, and Robin's. Such strong magic, and from a human child! Imagine what you could do if you were properly trained."

Emily gazed out at the fairy lady, her mind full of star-shine. Anstis was so beautiful. Emily had some vague thought that she wasn't always, that she'd seen the fairy look different, somehow. But it was hard to keep that in her mind, with the glittering figure smiling down at her so lovingly.

Anstis reached out one slim white hand and beckoned to her gently. "Come with me, Emily. I'll show you." She stepped back a little, and Emily could see the fairy world through the open doorway. It was a pleasure garden – the gardens that surrounded the king's palace. She had seen them once before, but she couldn't quite remember how. Her memories were blurred, and not really important anyway. . . There was a fountain playing now, and the water glittered like the stars. Emily leaned a little out of the window, staring towards the water, and gasped. She had seen water-sprites before, of course. She'd even met one, she seemed to remember. But not like this. As the veils of water from the fountain shimmered down, tiny, delicate creatures shot through them, riding the droplets and laughing gleefully as they cascaded into the gleaming stone basin.

"So pretty. . ." Emily murmured, leaning towards the glittering water.

"Even prettier close up," Anstis whispered

76

back, stretching out her hand again. "Take my hand. I can show you so many beautiful things, Emily. You have no idea. You can be a part of it all with me. You will belong." And just for a second, her whisper sharpened, and she almost hissed, "You'll belong, the way you never can at home. Come with me. Just step out."

"But I can't." Emily frowned. She had caught a touch of anger, and bitterness, behind the sweet words. "I'm not supposed to go. It's not safe."

Anstis showed her teeth as her sweet smile widened to a grimace. But then she recovered herself and laughed, like a gentle peal of little bells. "Who told you that, Emily? Your . . . *family*? But they would say that, wouldn't they?"

Emily shook her head. That glimpse of long

white teeth had bothered her, and there were strange blank patches in her head, as if someone had been messing around inside. "I don't understand," she whispered.

"They're trying to keep you away, sweetheart. They want you safe and sound on their side of the doors, where they can keep you under control."

"Under control?" Emily faltered.

"So they can use your power for themselves."

Emily laughed. She had seen Lark and Lory and Robin do magic, and even they were hundreds of times more powerful than she was – and that was nothing to what her parents could do. "They don't need me!" she said, shaking her head, and then her voice wobbled and her eyes filled with tears.

"So why do you stay?" Anstis purred. "Come

with me and you can have a real home. We'll look after you so well, Emily. *We* will love you."

"They do love me. . ." Emily tried to say, but it was so hard to fight against the choking sweetness of the fairy's voice.

"Poor dear thing." Anstis reached out her hand again. "They've lied to you so often, haven't they?"

Emily blinked at her, and then her eyes slid down to the reaching hand, the skin pale, the fingers so eager and clawlike. "It wasn't a lie," she said, more strongly this time. The blurry feeling in her head was lifting a little, as if someone was tearing away a veil of dust and cobwebs. She could see Lory sitting next to her at the kitchen table and rolling her hazel eyes at Emily's awful spelling. She could taste the sweetness of that

79

biscuit, and feel the intricate icing melting on her tongue – and she sniggered, suddenly realizing that it had been a spell to help her spell.

"What is it?" Lady Anstis demanded sharply. "Why are you laughing?" Her teeth were showing again, and Emily's eyes widened. Why had she believed her? She *knew* that Anstis was cruel and deceitful and desperate to steal a human child, so that she and her gang of fairy nobles could feed off the life and energy a human would bring them. A human child brought up in a fairy house was like pink iced doughnuts to Anstis.

But she was so *clever*. She knew all the little ways in. All the tricks. She had sensed Emily's misery, and worked on it so carefully.

"You knew," she said, looking clear-eyed at the

80

fairy at last. "You waited until I was upset, and then you sneaked in." Emily ground her teeth. "Well, I was stupid enough to let you, I suppose. But you're wrong, and I know you're wrong. They do love me!"

Lady Anstis stared down at her – she seemed taller now, and thinner. She had shrunk herself down before, so as to look more gentle, Emily decided.

"How could they?" she asked contemptuously. "You're a human."

She didn't need to say, *You're nothing*, but Emily knew that was what she meant. Her certainty rolled over Emily in a cold wave – that she was nothing, that she was unimportant, that she would never belong.

But then a tiny creature with dusty cocoa-coloured fur scurried along the window sill inside her head. Emily heard Robin calling crossly, *Come back! Brownie, where are you? You stupid mouse, that white monster of a cat'll have you for breakfast if you're not careful.*

Emily had made Brownie. She had made him, and Robin loved him. He loved her too, even if he hadn't thought she could do proper magic. She'd shown him, and he'd been pleased for her! And he'd come to find her after the argument with Eva, to see if she needed him.

Anstis was wrong.

"And even if you were right, and they don't love me, I'd still never go with you," Emily snarled angrily.

Lady Anstis swirled her star-white skirts around her, and the door in the air shut with a snap.

Emily woke up.

It was just getting light, and she was on the window sill, and the window was wide open – too open. She was dangerously close to falling out. "I thought that most of me was still in bed," Emily muttered, glancing back towards the sleeping bag and wondering if this was just another complicated layer of dream.

"You were, until she showed you the fountain. When you almost took her hand. Then she nearly had all of you."

Emily grabbed at the curtains, panicked and breathing fast. Then she peered round sideways and saw that Robin was sitting on the metal fire escape just outside the window.

"What are you doing here?" Emily muttered.

83

"I followed you when you didn't come back. Mum said you were having a sleepover, but. . ." He trailed off. "I was worried about you," he added, very quietly.

"Do I have a scent, then?" Emily asked. "You tracked me?"

"Yeah. And I knew where you were going, that helped," Robin admitted. "Um, are you coming home?" He looked at her sideways, and Emily's heart jumped. He was worried! He was frightened that she'd run away from home! He didn't want her to go!

"Because I'm really hungry," Robin added hopefully.

5

"I don't think this is a very good idea." Sasha was sitting hunched up on a mossy rock by the edge of her pond. It was *definitely* getting bigger, Emily decided. It hadn't had rocks all round it like that before. Emily scowled. She was furious with herself, for giving in to Anstis's magic so easily. How could she have forgotten Sasha, the water sprite that she knew best?

Sasha shook her head doubtfully, peering at Robin and Emily with pale green eyes. "It's dangerous."

"What is?" Emily demanded. "Robin, aren't you supposed to be nice to me right now? Tell me what's going on!"

But Robin didn't seem to be listening. He shrugged at Sasha. "We have to. She'll never settle otherwise, will she?"

"Don't call me 'she'!" Emily said crossly.

Sasha stretched out one foot and dabbled her toes in the water, as though it helped her think. "All right," she said at last. "I'll watch for you, then. I'll try and call you back, if anything goes wrong."

"What?" Emily squeaked. "Where are we going? What's happening?"

Robin stood up and grabbed her hand, hauling

her after him. "We're going to see what might have been," he told her. "So you can know." He dashed into the house with Emily stumbling behind and panting out questions.

"What might have been? I don't understand! And why are we going upstairs?"

"Because you keep opening doors on the stairs!" Robin told her swinging her round the corner of the landing and on to the rickety old staircase that led to Emily's attic room. "This is one of the easiest places to get through now, apart from Dad's proper entrances. Um. . ." He frowned, trying to think how to explain. "It's like there's a wall between here and the fairy world, and you've weakened it. And even though the fairy world's not where we're going, it's still easier to go to other places from this weak spot than anywhere else. So shut up and keep still, I have to think."

Emily opened her mouth to argue, but Robin had his eyes closed, and his face was empty. She wasn't sure he would even hear her any more. And then the dusty steps shimmered and shifted, and there was a dry scent of earth and a cold wind spilling around them. A crack of light shone through from somewhere else as the painted wall of the stairway tore and flapped open like the thick canvas of a tent. Emily swallowed and gripped Robin's hand tighter – and then he pulled, whisking her through the narrow gap in the wall. She glanced back, frightened, and reached for the familiar stairs again, but the dim staircase had gone. They fell tumbling over and over, on to something soft and rustling.

Leaves, Emily realized a moment later, when she dared to open her eyes. Dry, fallen leaves. They were in a wood. But not the fairy forest she had visited before, which had been lush and green and lovely. Here it seemed to be autumn, maybe winter. The trees were dropping their leaves, the branches almost bare. They made a dark net across the clear hard blue of the sky.

"Where are we?" Emily whispered. She didn't want to talk out loud, not here. There was something about the quiet lines of black trees that scared her.

"Nowhere. This is in the middle of lots of places." Robin got up slowly, staring around. "Um. Like a station platform? It's somewhere to go to the other places from."

Emily stared at him. "You mean there are doors to other places in the house too? Not just doors to your fairy world?"

"Not other places," Robin repeated patiently. "Here. Here's where you can get to the other places from."

"Where are we going?" Emily whispered, so quietly that Robin had to lean towards her to hear. "You said we were going to see what might have been. I don't understand."

Robin sighed. "Ever since you found out you had another family, you've been thinking about them, haven't you? You want to know what it would have been like if your real parents had kept you."

"Yes," Emily admitted, kicking at the dry leaves with the toe of her plimsoll. She felt ashamed, after the way her adopted family had been so kind to her. She was so *lucky*! Why couldn't she just accept things as they were? But even though she loved them all, so much, she still wanted to know about her real parents. She was sure that meeting them, even just *seeing* them, would tell her something about herself.

"So that's what we're going to find out. You've got to know. Come on." He grabbed at her and started to lead her through the dark trees.

"But we can't! It never happened, so how can we go there? I don't understand! Stop pulling me!"

"Fine," Robin snapped. And he let go of her.

Emily was about to complain that he'd hurt her wrist, although he hadn't really, when her grumpy voice seemed to catch in her throat. All she said was, "Oh. . ." in a sort of muffled squeak.

The strange wood wasn't there any more. Robin had pulled her out of it, as easily as he had dragged her in. And then he'd let her go. Not caring if it made her look silly, Emily reached back and caught his hand again, in her own cold one. Somehow, they were indoors again – but not in their own sweet-smelling, dusty old house. Robin had taken her somewhere different. Somewhere she had never been.

"Where is this?" she whispered. "What have you done?"

Robin sighed and rolled his eyes, but even he looked rather nervous. "We're here," he murmured. "Look. You have to go through that door. I'll wait for you."

Emily gulped, but the place didn't look frightening. It was just a house, as far as she could tell. A landing with a slightly faded carpet and a basket of folded washing. She did as she was told, slipping around the door of a small room – not all that different from her own bedroom at home. But pinker. As though it had been decorated for a little girl and left the same, even though the girl had grown up.

A teenage girl was sitting on the bed in the corner of the room, leaning back against the wall and staring down at a flimsy piece of paper in her hands. Her hair had fallen forward over her face, so it was hard to see what she looked like, but Emily was almost sure that the girl was her mother.

Forgetting to worry about how she'd managed to

get there, or whether it was safe, or if anyone could see her, Emily ghosted over towards the bed and sat down next to the girl. She looked older than Lark and Lory, Emily thought, but not that much older. Sixteen? Seventeen? The girl was crying, Emily realized now that she was closer. She was staring down at the piece of paper and silently crying, tears just running down the sides of her nose without stopping, more and more of them.

Emily peered at the piece of paper, trying to work out what it was. The paper was scruffy and smudged, but then the girl ran her hand over it to smooth it out, stroking her fingers over it so gently. And Emily saw that it was a face. A baby's face, tiny and perfect. It was a drawing of Emily, from before she was born. Her mother's idea of what she might look like.

94

All at once, Emily was sure. This wasn't what might have been – this was real. This had actually happened. This was her mother, young and frightened, in her little-girly pink bedroom.

Emily edged closer to her mother. She *wanted* the girl to see her this time. If she saw Emily, then perhaps they could talk to each other. Her mother would be able to explain. . .

Although, actually, just being there in that pretty pink room explained quite a lot. Seeing the girl's face streaked with tears, seeing her so scared. She wasn't ready to be a mother.

Emily leaned herself cautiously against the girl's shoulder, wondering if she would be able to feel that Emily was there. Hoping that somehow she would know.

95

The girl lifted her head a little and rubbed at her shoulder. Emily guessed that maybe she thought a fly or something had landed there. The girl's fingers tickled Emily a little as they swept over her face, and she could obviously feel Emily too. She sprang sideways with a sharp cry, pressing herself into the corner of the wall.

"What is it? Who's there?" she whispered, holding out her hand and sweeping it in front of her to see if she could feel anything.

Emily pressed her own fingers against the older girl's. Her mother's hand was almost the same size as her own.

Emily couldn't help thinking of Eva and how different she was to her real mother. Her pregnancy was making her more beautiful than ever – her red hair was thicker and longer and shinier than it had ever been, and her skin looked golden. But then, Eva was a fairy, and she had Ash to look after her. And a house, and a family of other children – even if they weren't being very nice to her at the moment. Eva had so much family around her, but it seemed that this girl was all alone, in her little pink room, with no one to talk to.

Gently, she pressed her fingers against her mother's again, hoping that she would push back, like a message.

"Who are you?" the girl whispered again, but she didn't take her hand away.

Emily gulped. "Emily. . ." she whispered back. Her voice came out strange, like an echo, and she wasn't sure if her mother would hear her. But the girl blinked, looking around in bewilderment.

"What's your name?" Emily asked suddenly. She hadn't realized until now that she had no idea what her mother's name was.

The girl swallowed and closed her eyes, as if to make herself feel braver. "Izzy. . ." she murmured. "Are you a ghost?"

Emily laughed, and she felt the laugh tremble through her fingertips and reach out to Izzy. Her mother.

The older girl's cheeks grew pinker, as though some of Emily's strength had gone into her with that little laugh. She stopped crying, and wrapped her cold fingers around Emily's own. "Maybe you're not a ghost – I can almost feel that you're really there. Almost." She squeezed Emily's hand tighter, and with her other hand she reached up, as if she wanted to stroke Emily's hair. "There's something so familiar about you." Then she gave a little gasp. "You're the baby, aren't you?" Izzy whispered, drawing her hand away and wrapping her arms over her stomach.

"I think so. . ."

Izzy looked up, and her eyes were shiny and wet with tears again. "I suppose you're just my imagination," she muttered. "Because I'm not sleeping much. But it doesn't feel like I've made you up. I didn't know this is what you'd look like."

"It's funny, I'm not sure if I'm making you up either," Emily told her, and Izzy's mouth twisted just a little, into an almost-smile. She moved her hand again, reaching out for Emily's, and Emily took it gratefully. Izzy shivered as she felt Emily's fingers touch hers. "I'm sorry," she whispered. "I don't know what to do. I can't have a baby. I want to. But I can't. I just can't. . ."

Emily swallowed. "It's all right," she managed to say, her voice croaky and strangled suddenly. And it was.

She'd never thought it could be, but it was. Izzy was terrified. She was too young. She was sure she couldn't look after a baby Emily.

"You *could* look after me," Emily told her shakily. "You could try. Some people do, even when they're as young as you, and they're good at it. Really good. But it's all right. That's what I came to say, I think. I'll be all right. Probably better, if you let me go."

It was true, and somehow it helped to say it.

"I hope you'll be all right too. . ." Emily whispered, gently taking her hand out of her mother's. She was going – she could feel it, the pull of home. Her real home. It was stronger than Izzy's frightened, shiny eyes, and the pink bedroom. Emily was going back home. It *was* her true home, just as she'd angrily told Lady Anstis. Now she was sure.

The trees of the between-place blurred past her, and Emily smiled, reaching out towards home, and her brother and sisters, her father and mother. Especially Eva. Seeing Izzy had made her feel desperately sorry for her real mother, but it had also made Emily realize how much she loved Eva, and how much Eva loved her, and always had. Emily wanted to get home, and tell her that she knew now. She needed her.

And then someone lifted her up and hugged her, just like she always used to when Emily fell.

"Mum! How did you get here?" Emily muttered into Eva's shoulder. "I was with Robin. I think. . . And then. . ." She looked up, blinking anxiously. "He's still there! Mum, I left him behind!"

Eva shook her head. "It's all right. He's in the garden. When I saw what you were doing, I brought him home, and I waited for you instead. Oh, Emily, I missed you!"

"I know." Emily nodded. She was safe, and so was Robin, and she was home. They were in Eva's workroom now, she realized dazedly. Curled up in the battered old armchair in the corner.

"You called me, Emily. I felt it. I should have been here before, I'm sorry. I was so caught up with the baby, I thought you were just being grumpy and jealous like Lory. I didn't realize. That you thought I'd stop loving you. Or how upset you were."

"I'm not now. I understand. But I was so selfish about the baby. . ." Emily whispered apologetically. "I felt horrible."

Eva sighed. "We didn't tell you very well. I'm sorry, Emily. I know it's hard for you."

"I don't feel like that now. . ."

Eva kissed her cheek, and Emily sighed, feeling her mother's fairy magic. Instead of settling over her skin, it seemed to rush right through her, filling Emily with a sense of love and belonging that she'd never understood before.

"Maybe I was right to go away," she murmured. "If you don't ever go away, you can't come home."

6

"That's beautiful," Emily murmured, admiring the design in the sketch pad laid out on Eva's table. Ivy leaves in shades of green and black and silver wound across the page, and as Emily watched, the silvery lines twisted and shimmered, and tiny creatures seemed to peer out from between the winding stems, grinning at her.

"It's a design for a silk scarf," Eva explained,

flicking her fingers and sending the little sprites running back into the paint. "Though of course, the scarf won't have the added extras. . . You really must be getting stronger, Emily, now that you can see the magic in my designs." She shook up the cushions on the little sofa in the corner of her studio and gently pushed Emily on to it. "You look exhausted," she told Emily, lowering herself down carefully next to her.

Eva was looking a lot bigger, Emily suddenly thought, noticing the careful way she moved. She was still graceful, but it was a watchful, considered sort of grace, nothing like her usual dancing movement.

"Are you all right?" Emily asked anxiously, sitting up again. She had slumped back against the cushions, tired out after her strange day. A dozen different odd things had happened to her since she'd found out the truth about her family. But the journey into another version of her own life had been the strangest of all. At the same time, Emily was happier than she had been for ages. She was sure now that she belonged here – not with Izzy. She felt peaceful, she decided, now that she knew more about her birth mother. Peaceful, but also a bit limp and exhausted. Still, she struggled upright, looking worriedly at her mother.

"Oh, I'm fine!" Eva smiled at her. "Just so clumsy and big. Sit back, Emily." Her voice was very soft now, with a low buzz to it like the hum of a bumblebee, and Emily smiled.

"Did you do this when I was a baby?" she

106

murmured. "Sing spells to me, to send me to sleep?"

"Sometimes," her mother said, laughing. "But you were never that much of a problem to get to sleep. I should think you remember me singing to Robin – he didn't want to sleep at all."

Emily nodded. "I wonder what the new baby will be like. . ." she said drowsily, leaning her head against Eva's shoulder.

"Me too," her mother whispered, stroking her fingers gently down Emily's cheek. The buzzing seemed to fill the room – a soft, sleepy, musical sound. It purred in and out of Emily's mind, making her think of sunshine, and humming bees, and honey sweetness. And cats, just for a moment, which made her twitch crossly, thinking of Dantis and his smug white-catness. The humming of the spell deepened, and pulled her further into sleep.

Emily began to dream. She was restless at first, wriggling and tossing her head, and Eva patted her hair, smoothing it down gently and changing the note of the humming magic that was keeping Emily asleep. Emily shifted herself, snuggling more comfortably against Eva's shoulder, and settled into a deeper, quieter sleep. Her dreams were pleasanter ones now – dreams of fairy babies, smiling and clapping their hands. One of them patted its fat little hand against hers, over and over again, fascinated that Emily's hands were so much larger than its own. *Her* own. It was a little girl. Emily didn't know much about babies, but even she could tell that. The baby's soft yellow wings fluttered in her excitement, nearly tipping her over. That made her laugh even more. Emily caught her, ready to set her upright, but she giggled and fluttered and stumbled into the air, bumbling around Emily in giddy little swoops. Her dark eyes were fixed on Emily, and she kept darting down and patting at Emily's hair, stroking the curls, just as Eva had been doing.

Eva. . . Emily blinked, and stretched herself awake, yawning deliciously and looking up at her mother with sleepy eyes.

Eva looked as though she might have been asleep too. Her face was pale, and her eyes looked heavy.

Emily stroked her hand, smiling. "I was dreaming about babies."

Eva blinked and tried to smile. "That's strange,

so was I," she said lightly, but Emily could hear the strained note in her voice.

"What's the matter?" she asked anxiously, and then she saw how Eva was pressing her hands against her bump, smoothing the wrinkled fabric of her dress over and over again. "Oh! Is it the baby? Is it coming?" *She*, something inside her said firmly. *You saw her. It was a girl.* "Is she coming?" Emily asked again, and Eva nodded.

"I think so. Come with me, Emily." She pushed herself up awkwardly from the sofa, and held out one hand.

"Where are we going?" Emily asked, frowning. "The hospital?" She knew that was where babies were usually born, but somehow she hadn't thought Eva would want to go there. Wouldn't a fairy birth be different from a human one? *Especially with those pretty little yellow wings.* Emily blinked. Had she dreamed about her own new baby sister? Before she was even born? She looked thoughtfully at Eva's bump. Perhaps fairy babies could do magic even in the womb. Emily was almost sure her little sister had sent the dream. *She knows me*, Emily thought, a sudden gladness spilling over inside her. *And I've seen those yellow feathers before*, she realized. *When I was close to Mum. She was there, the baby! She's been trying to talk to me all this time!*

"No, not the hospital." Eva grimaced, her shoulders hunching for a moment, and then beckoned to Emily, more urgently this time. "We're going back home. The baby needs to be

111

born at home. Through the doors."

"Is it safe?" Emily murmured, thinking of Lady Anstis. Then she shook her head. Of course it was, if she went with Eva. Her mother was a lady of the fairy court too, even if she lived in the human world most of the time. The other fairy ladies might sniff around them, jealous of the delicious energy they could sense in Emily, a human child, but Eva would be with her. Eva would never let anyone steal her away.

"Which door shall we go through?" Emily whispered. "And aren't we going to fetch any of the others? Dad? Lark and Lory?"

"Your dad will come, don't worry. He'll bring the others. But I need to go now, Emily, and I want you with me. You dreamed about

112

the baby, didn't you?"

Emily stared at her. "With the little yellow wings?" she asked at last. "Was that really her?"

Eva smiled, even though she still looked as though she was hurting. "Your little sister." She shook her head. "It seems to me she's going to be even more of a nightmare baby than Robin. At least he wasn't born flying. Come on, Emily." She took Emily's hand. "I have my own door."

Eva led Emily to the table, which was scattered with her designs, tiny pieces of fabric, art materials, and the odd mug of cold tea here and there. She flipped open a sketchbook and propped herself against the table with a sigh. Then she snatched up a chalk pastel crayon and began to draw with long, sweeping strokes. She sketched in the lines of a doorway, and Emily watched in wonder as it seemed to stand out of the page.

Coiling up beyond the doorway was a staircase, a spiral one, with deep treads that twirled on upwards. Emily blinked, following the steps with her eyes as they seemed to continue beyond the edge of the paper.

The magic helped, of course, but most of the life in the drawing came from her mother's confident lines. After a minute's sketching, she stood back, smiled a little and blew across the page.

Emily watched a haze of bluish chalk dust lift and shimmer in the air above the drawing, twinkling like starlight around the stairs. While she was distracted by the dust motes, the door itself lifted out of the page, so that it was suddenly there in front of her.

It didn't make sense – the doorway was standing there, clear and solid, with the silvery steps spiralling beyond it. And yet the table was still there too, heavy and wooden, just as it had been before. Emily squinted. They were both there at the same time, which shouldn't have been possible, but it was.

Emily sucked in a breath as they took their first step through the doorway and on to the stairs, and the stars glimmered around them. They were painted on to a plastered wall, and yet they seemed real, glowing in some far-away night that stood between the worlds.

They walked up slowly, hand in hand, until they came to a door of silvery, weathered wood, with a

115

barley sugar twisted ring of dull black metal for a handle. Eva shivered a little as she touched it, and smiled down at Emily. "Cold iron. It's hard for us to touch. Crossing between our worlds should never be too easy."

Emily nodded, but she was finding it hard to concentrate on her mother's words. It seemed so long since she had been in the fairy world, even though it was only a few weeks. And she had never been there with Eva. This was no panicked, mistaken dash through a door that had been left ajar. She hadn't forced her way in, breaking all the rules. She was visiting for real. She was *allowed*.

Beyond the doorway was a stone-floored passageway, hung with tapestries and rich embroidered hangings that sparkled and moved like Eva's designs. Butterflies spiralled dizzily across stitched meadows in front of her, and a petal fell from a heavy, sweet-perfumed rose. Emily breathed in the honey sweetness of the flower and reached out to cup its petals, but Eva gently pulled her away.

"There's no time, Emily love. If you fall in among those flowers, you won't want to leave. This way. . ."

She led Emily up the passageway to another heavy wooden door, so much like the one she had drawn that Emily looked back, only to find that the wall opposite the embroidered roses was bare stone. The door had slipped away as soon as Eva closed it behind them.

But the handle on this door was a soft, rich

117

gold, and it was warm when Emily reached out to open it for her mother. The room inside seemed familiar, even though Emily was sure she had never been in it before. Eva had decorated it, she realized, and the hangings and paintings made her think of their home in the human world.

Eva curled up in a strange high-backed chair, which Emily didn't think looked very comfortable, but she sighed happily as she wriggled her spine against the bumpy wooden carvings. "Better. . ." she murmured, closing her eyes. Then they flickered open again for a moment as she told Emily, "Stay here, in this room. I mean it, Emily. Don't go out."

Emily sniffed. "After last time? I don't want to be bewitched into staying here for ever." She gripped the back of her mother's chair tightly. Would she be able to resist Anstis again? Would she know the deceitful magic for what it was? She hoped so, but she didn't mean to risk it. "I'm staying with you." She looked at Eva a little worriedly. "Does anyone here know that we're here, if you see what I mean? People like Lady Anstis?"

"Yes. . ." Eva nodded fractionally. She wasn't really concentrating on what Emily was saying – she was thinking about the baby. Emily wondered how close it was to happening. She wished her dad were here.

"Anstis will know – she has spies everywhere. And others may have felt the door open, too. . ."

Emily flinched as the door flew open and banged, echoing against the stone wall. She wasn't

119

sure who she had been expecting, but she let out a gasp of relief when her father strode into the room and crouched before Eva's chair.

"You're all right?" he asked her anxiously. "And the baby?"

Eva chuckled. "She spoke to us – to me and Emily. She has yellow wings. Ohhh. . ." She moaned, and grimaced, and Ash gathered her up into his arms and carried her through another door into what Emily assumed was a bedroom. She wondered if they needed a midwife, or someone to help, but her father glanced back over his shoulder and smiled at her. "Just stay there, Emily. And don't worry."

Emily nodded, even though she thought it was a stupid thing to say. How could she not worry? And the way both her parents had been so insistent that she stayed in the room was daunting too. If she'd been Lory, she'd probably have marched straight out into the passage and gone looking for trouble. But Emily wasn't like that at all. She was desperate to explore, but she'd settle for looking around the family's rooms.

There were several other doors, she realized now. Bedrooms for Lark and Lory and Robin, she guessed. She peeped into one of them, but it was very bare – almost empty, with just a bed and a huge mirror on the wall. Her brother and sisters had never lived here. Emily grinned to herself as she saw a piece of Lego sticking out from underneath the bed by the wall, and she darted into the room to pick it up, comforted by this little trace of Robin.

She knelt down to pull it out, and then scurried back on her knees in panic as a heavy black paw smacked down in front of her, shiny claws dragging back the plastic brick. A low growl echoed out from under the bed, and Emily whimpered. There was a monster under the bed! It was the sort of thing she'd dreamed about when she was smaller, so she'd never wanted to reach her hand out of the covers in case something bit her, and now it was actually happening.

But then the black dog wriggled himself out from under the bed and stared at her. He looked guilty.

"Gruff! Oh! You scared me!" Emily gasped. "Did you come with us? Why are you hiding? Aren't you supposed to be here?"

She wasn't expecting him to answer – after all, he never had when she'd spoken to him before. But he lowered his great head in a nod and eyed her sideways. "I came to protect Lady Eva," he rumbled, and Emily gaped at him.

"You talk. . ." she faltered.

"Here I do."

Emily bit her lip, thinking of all the times she had curled up next to him and told him how unfair Lark and Lory were, or how much Robin was annoying her with stupid boy tricks. "And, um, do you understand what people are saying when we're at home?"

Gruff's dark, almond-shaped eyes glittered for a moment, and Emily knew that he did.

"Oh." She frowned. "That isn't very fair. That's

the sort of thing you ought to tell people."

"A little sign on my collar, perhaps?" He nudged his huge head against hers, and she could feel that he was laughing. He quivered with it.

Emily sighed. "I'm glad you're here. I'm sure Mum's all right, but it's eerie, that shut door, and just hearing noises every so often. And I keep expecting someone to charge in and tell me I shouldn't be here."

"Two of us, then." The great dog stood up, and Emily laid her hand on his neck and let him lead her out into the main room. They stood by the windows, looking out at a view of dark, distant mountains, and Emily was glad to have the warmth of his fur under her hand. The mountains made her think of dwarves, or maybe trolls. She

124

dragged her eyes away from their forbidding bulk, and stared down at the pretty pleasure gardens just below the window instead. Several people were strolling there in the sunshine, and Emily watched them curiously.

The women's glittering dresses and folded wings reminded her of Anstis and the other Ladies, and her first journey through the doors. She shivered. Gruff shifted, and Emily blinked as he grew taller, and wider at the shoulders. His collar had spikes on it, she noticed. She was sure it hadn't had them before. He looked like a bear. "No one will harm you," he told Emily grimly, and she believed him.

"Why would anyone want to harm her?" a sweet voice asked.

Emily swallowed painfully and turned, forcing

herself to loosen her grip on Gruff's black fur. She had dug her nails into his back so hard it must have hurt. But he only nudged her affectionately, never taking his eyes from the woman standing in the doorway.

"How nice to see you again, dear child." Lady Anstis smiled at Emily charmingly, and Emily fought to keep the charm from seeping through her defences. "And on such a happy occasion."

"You know about the baby?" Emily gasped, looking anxiously towards her mother's door.

"But of course. Everyone knows. Fairy children are rare, and special." Anstis was smiling, but her smile looked unpleasantly greedy to Emily. She was wearing green velvet this time, and it looked softer than the dust on her drooping butterfly wings. Emily felt a deep longing inside her to reach out and stroke the dress, perhaps curl up at Anstis's feet, and lean her head against the pale velvet.

Don't! Emily wasn't sure if that had come from Gruff, or her own sense of self-preservation. But she stepped back sharply and stared at her feet, so as not to see the fairy Lady smile. Emily pressed herself closer to Gruff. "Did you come to see my mother?" she asked, trying not to let her voice shake.

"Of course." Anstis was laughing, and her voice was a purr. "Give her my good wishes, Emily, won't you? Tell her I will visit soon. So I can meet the child." She stalked out, and Emily stood still for a moment, and then raced across the room to shut the door and lean against it, gasping.

"I don't want her to see the baby!" she told Gruff. "She mustn't. She's poisonous, can't you feel it?"

But Gruff was gazing fixedly at the other door now, his ears pricked up. He pawed the ground with one front foot, and then paced across the room.

Emily hurried after him. "Has it happened?" she whispered, but he didn't seem to be listening to her. Emily frowned, trying to hear what the huge dog could hear, and then through the wooden panels came a thin, cross wail, and Emily knew that Wren had been born.

7

Emily reached out to the door, desperate to meet her little sister, but then she drew her hand back. She couldn't just walk in, but something – someone – inside the room was calling her. Yellow-gold feathers fluttered and swooped inside her, and she could almost see them out of the corner of her eye.

"It's Wren," Gruff agreed, lifting a massive paw

and scratching firmly at the wooden panels. "She sounds most determined about it. Ah!" He nosed forward curiously as the door swung open, and Emily followed him.

Her mother was leaning back against a pile of pillows, her red hair streaming down on to the covers and coiling around the baby in her arms. She smiled at Emily, hesitating in the doorway. "Come and see," she whispered. "Come and see her."

The baby wriggled and cooed, and waved a fat hand imperiously at Emily.

"Climb up here," Eva murmured, patting the embroidered coverlet next to her.

Emily looked a little uncertainly at her dad, who was sitting on the edge of the bed. She didn't want to hurt Eva. But he nodded, and Gruff nudged her forward. The big dog peered at the baby too.

"I should have known you'd find your way here," Eva said, smiling at him. "I didn't think, or I'd have called you myself."

Emily climbed up on to the bed. She could feel the baby like a little fire burning, spreading warmth across the whole room. There was so much magic bubbling out of her. Emily leaned over to look into her face, expecting a little blonde child, like a miniature Lark or Lory, or perhaps a china-pale baby with Eva's red hair. But the baby's hair was dark, and she stared up at Emily with velvety brown eyes.

"She looks like you," Ash said, smiling at Emily.

Emily frowned. "But she can't. And shouldn't

131

her eyes be blue? Oh, I suppose fairy babies aren't all born with blue eyes."

"She can look like you if she wants to," Eva said fondly. "She knows you, Emily, look."

It was true that the baby seemed to be reaching for Emily with her little stubby hands, and Emily leaned close and let the child wind eager fingers into her long dark curls.

"Don't pull, little one," Ash murmured. "Treat your sister gently."

The baby seemed to understand, for she stopped grabbing and simply beamed at Emily. She was bigger and far more awake-looking than any human newborn, Emily thought. She already seemed to understand what was happening around her, and who her family were.

"How long must we stay?" Eva asked Ash tiredly. "I don't want. . . You know. . ."

Emily looked up sharply, intercepting the meaningful look between her parents.

"What is it?" she asked, putting out a protective hand towards the baby. Nothing was going to happen to her little sister. Gruff was pressing closer against the bed too, and the fur had lifted round his neck and all along his spine, making him look more bear-like than ever. Emily could feel the baby's warm magic. It wrapped around Emily like a young plant, growing and twining in and out of all of her. Emily frowned at her mum and dad. "Is something the matter? Is it something to do with Wren?"

"How did you. . .?" her father began, as her mother said, "Wren! She's Wren!"

133

"She told me," Emily agreed. "But what did you mean before? Is something wrong?"

"Fairy babies are rare, you see," her father said slowly. "There may be . . . interest . . . in Wren."

Emily gasped. She had forgotten! "Lady Anstis! She knows already; she came here. Just before we heard Wren cry. She said she wanted to visit you and meet the child," she added to Eva. "I don't think you should let her see Wren, Mum, she's so creepy."

Eva started to sit up, and she lifted the baby gently and held her out to Emily. "You hold her. We have to go. And it isn't Wren that Anstis wants," she said to Ash. "It's Emily she's really after. I shouldn't have brought her here. But I wanted her with me. And so did Wren," she added, smiling at Emily. "She made it very clear that I was to bring you too."

134

Emily gripped Wren tightly – too tightly, in her panic that she might drop the tiny thing. A small pink fist flailed out and smacked her arm, and the baby wriggled crossly. Emily gasped in delight, forgetting to worry about marauding fairy Ladies as the golden-yellow wings fluttered determinedly out of the blankets round her baby sister. They were still tiny – smaller than they had been in Emily's dream – but it was clear that it wouldn't be long before they could lift Wren into the air.

"Don't fly away just yet," Emily told her seriously. "We have to get home first. It isn't safe here."

A deep curiosity about home welled up inside her from the baby, and she smiled down at Wren. "You'll like it," she promised. "You've got other sisters too – and Robin; he's your brother. He's funny."

Ash helped Eva out of bed and wrapped a velvet cloak around her shoulders. He took another one from a wooden chest under the windows and swathed Emily in it, so that the baby was half-hidden under the soft, heavy folds. Then he led them out into the main room, with Gruff pacing close behind.

It was then that someone banged on the door, loud enough that Eva gasped and went pale. Ash whisked round, snatching the cloak from Emily and gently pushing her and Eva into the tall wooden chairs, and then went to the door. Emily could see him lifting his chin and drawing back his shoulders as he walked, and his bearing was lord-like as he flung the door open.

"My lady." He swept Lady Anstis a bow, and

she curtseyed back to him gracefully, although Emily thought she was annoyed to see him there. Perhaps she'd hoped that Eva and Emily had come alone. There were several other fairy women with her, and Emily wrapped her arms around Wren a little more tightly as she recognized them. These were the Ladies from Anstis's rooms, the ones who had tried to feed her fairy fruit and keep her here. Their faces were still beautiful, but Emily could see that they looked hungry, and jealous. All of them glanced curiously at the bundle of baby in her arms, but their greedy eyes kept returning to her own face.

Emily could feel the warm, solid weight of Wren pressed close against her. She knew that however upset she had been by the thought of a new baby, now that Wren was here, there was nothing she wouldn't do to protect her sister. She wasn't sure if Wren's magic would have this effect on everyone – that whoever saw the baby would love her and want to care for her – or if it was only Emily herself. But that didn't matter. The fairies weren't keeping Emily, or her little sister.

"So this is the child. . ." Lady Anstis murmured. "How very lovely, Eva. A precious treasure indeed." She leaned over Emily, reaching out a hand as though to touch the baby's cheek, and Emily cast a frantic glance at Ash. Was it all right to let Anstis touch Wren? Could she hurt her? Or put a spell on her, perhaps? Gruff was next to the chair, and even sitting, his great head was a on a level with the baby. Could he protect them from a spell?

138

Emily's father only smiled, and made a calming gesture with his hand, but the smile was forced. She could see that he was worried.

Then Anstis stepped back again, her hand stilled in the air above Wren's face. It was as though Wren herself had stopped her, Emily thought, looking down at the baby, who gazed back at her with night-dark eyes. Was she strong enough to stop Anstis already?

Anstis stood there for a second, her long hands clenched, and then she smiled over at Eva, a smile even more forced than Ash's had been. "You have such a large family now." She looked Emily up and down, and added, "And so unusual," in a flat sort of tone which Emily was absolutely certain was supposed to be rude.

Eva was still sitting, her arms stretched along the wooden arms of the chair as though she were on a throne. She didn't even bother smiling. "Indeed," she agreed. "Thank you, Lady Anstis, for visiting us – so soon after the birth, too." Eva stood up and swept her cloak around her shoulders again. She looked almost completely recovered, Emily thought. "We are returning home now, to rest, and for our new daughter to meet the others of our family."

"Already?" Anstis moved to the chair opposite Eva, and sat down, the other Ladies gathering themselves around her in a practised sort of pose. "We were so hoping that you'd stay longer."

"We?" Ash asked sharply, as Eva settled unwillingly back into her chair.

Lady Anstis smiled, and stroked the green velvet

folds of her skirt. "As you know, our dear king so generously listens to my advice," she murmured, her voice so soft that Emily had to lean forward to listen. She could feel Wren tensing in her arms, watching the older fairy carefully. Was she old enough to understand what was happening already? Or was she simply picking up on the air of menace in the room?

"I have confided in him," Anstis went on slowly, "some of my concerns about your family. Your so unusual family. This child." She waved delicately at Emily. "A human, but *not*. Not any more. She has been changed, hasn't she?"

"You only think that because I wouldn't listen when you tried to bewitch me!" Emily snapped angrily.

Lady Anstis raised her eyebrows, as though she was shocked at such impolite behaviour, and Ash laid a restraining hand on Emily's shoulder.

"As you can see, she is – not under control," Anstis said disdainfully. "Given to angry outbursts. As one would expect, from a human child exposed to fairy magic. She is simply not meant to have such power. It may well send her mad, eventually."

"What nonsense!" Eva spat. "And Emily is very sensible. Far more so than our other children."

"Ah – but you see, she is not your child, is she? This is all some misguided form of affection for your little human pet. And without realizing it, you have let her into all sorts of secrets, given her spells to play with, turned her into some odd half-fairy thing. She is *wrong*. And she cannot be allowed back into the human world. She is too dangerous. She could hurt people. Or, worse, she could tell."

Emily shuddered. The fairy's voice was like ice. And even though she knew that Anstis was evil, and this was all about her taking Emily's power for her own, the picture she painted was frightening. Might she really go mad because of the fairy magic that had seeped inside her?

Eva wrapped an arm around her shoulders. "Don't listen," she whispered. And then she stood up and glared at Anstis. "This is a ridiculous power play," she announced in a voice that was just as icy. "Leave us. Now. We are taking our daughters home."

"No. She will stay."

Emily gasped as a spell swirled about her – how had Anstis cast it so suddenly? Unless it had been creeping around her since Anstis had entered the room. She had been talking to play for time, Emily realized, as she tried to tear at the magic with one hand. Whatever the spell was, it bound her tightly, so tightly she couldn't even squeak for help. And now it was making her walk, so that she tottered across the stone floor, fighting uselessly against her own body.

"Let go of her!" Eva screamed, and Emily stopped, gasping for breath. She was still bound, though – Ash and Eva hadn't managed to free her, though she could feel their magic, testing and pulling at the bonds, frantically teasing the spells away. But all the time Anstis was still working, wrapping her in more and more layers of magic. It was getting hard to breathe.

Emily looked down anxiously at Wren. The baby was so tiny, and she was imprisoned in the spell too. What if it hurt her?

Wren stared back at her, her dark eyes glinting like jewels. "It's all right," Emily tried to whisper, but no sound came out. "I'll look after you," she breathed, but it was a stupid thing to say. She couldn't look after anyone. The spell was so strong. Would Anstis let it choke her? Would she kill them if she couldn't have Emily for her own?

Wren screwed her eyes shut. Emily could feel her fat little fingers, pulling in Ash and Eva's magic and weaving it together with something childlike

145

and strong and very, very new. A magic that was all her own.

Threads of gold wound in and out of the choking magic now, glittering around Emily and Wren and easing the spell-bindings apart. Emily felt the tightness in her chest slip away, and she took a deep gasping breath. She hugged Wren tightly to her with one arm, and with the other she shoved the rest of the Anstis's magic away from herself and her little sister, so angrily that she staggered and half fell. A great, harsh tearing echoed through the room, and then a gentle pattering, like rain or falling leaves. Emily opened her eyes, and straightened up cautiously.

Anstis's spell had simply gone – leaving hundreds of threads of pinkish, fibrous stuff

146

littered around her feet. Emily stirred them with
her toe and flinched as they squirmed. She hadn't
realized that they were alive.

"How did you break the spell?" Emily murmured
to her sister as Eva snatched her and Wren out of
Anstis's reach and set them in the wooden chair,
with Gruff standing in front to guard them. The
huge dog was growling constantly on one low
note, a sound full of power and fury. Emily was
sure that growl would hurt anyone that came near.

Then Emily's parents paced towards Anstis,
moving together, step by step. Anstis was
surrounded by her companions, but one of them
was already backing away towards the door, and
Emily sensed that several of the others were
about to run too. Ash and Eva looked grand, and

fearsome, and terrifyingly angry. Ash was even less human-looking now, so tall, with his black eyes half filling his face and his long, long fingers outstretched towards the fairy Ladies.

Eva's cloak swirled around her as she walked, and it seemed to be alive, tiny creatures snarling and snapping as they raced around the folds, baring their teeth at Anstis. A tiny wolf ran up into Eva's hair and then leaned out to howl fury at the enemy.

As the two sides met, Emily turned her face away, burying it in Wren's blankets and wishing as hard as she ever had. *Let them be safe, let them be safe, let us all get home*. She could feel Gruff's growl deepening, and he shifted uneasily in front of them, wanting to dive in and join the fight. But his mistress had set him to guard, and he would.

Emily forced herself to look up – her parents were fighting for her, at least she could be brave enough to watch them.

Lady Anstis was fighting alone now; all her butterfly-winged companions had fled. Anstis herself looked different – older, Emily thought at first, and then she decided that it wasn't age, it was simply that the fairy was having to use all her magic to fight now. She had none to spare for the spells that made her beautiful. It was her real self that was tearing and clawing and kicking as Ash and Eva's magic fought her.

Emily watched her mother's hands winding together, the fingers twirling and lacing in a delicate pattern. She was drawing a spell together, shaping and weaving it into a thin, gauzy cloth, like

149

the designs she made at home in her workroom. Emily could see the spells shimmering inside it, flickering and moving like flames, and they leaped up high as Eva tossed the spell-cloth into the air. It floated slowly down, and Ash stretched out one hand, flicking his fingers at it lazily.

Emily leaned forward curiously. She had hardly ever seen her father do magic and didn't have much sense of his fairy power. She didn't really know what his magic *did*.

The words came out of nowhere. Fine and black, like a swarm of tiny bees, humming as they wrote themselves into Eva's magic in fragile scrolls and curls across the fabric. She should have realized, Emily thought. Even before she had understood what her family were, she had known that her father wrote about magic. She had always wondered how he thought up all those horrific monsters, not knowing that they were real, only somewhere else. Now she could see that he wrote his spells too. There was something everlasting about those black black words, something that made Emily sure that once caught, Anstis would never be able to break free.

Eva caught the silken spell as it floated down, and then she swirled it towards Anstis, who was already backing away, her eyes dark with horror. She could see the power of this magic that they were about to cast, a far stronger binding than the one she had used on Emily. But as she turned, flinging wild streams of magic at Ash and Eva, the very edge of the fabric flicked across her shoulder, and it had her. The gossamer silk settled softly, relentlessly, over her skin.

"What is it doing?" Emily murmured, but she didn't really expect anyone to answer her. She and Gruff and Wren were all staring at the spell, all struck silent by its unstoppable power. The spell-silk wrapped tighter and tighter around Anstis – Eva had chosen this spell on purpose, Emily was sure. Anstis had tried to hurt her and Wren with something so similar, this had to be a furious mother's revenge.

Anstis was still fighting, but her struggles were growing weaker and weaker, and Emily hated it. "Stop it!" she begged. "You're hurting her!"

There was a silence – no more growling, no more of Ash's gasping breaths, no shrieking from the wolf-cloak wrapped round Eva's shoulders.

Her mother glanced back and nodded. "I'm sorry, Emily. We don't have a choice." She made one more twisting movement, like tying a knot, and then she ripped her hands apart – and the spell broke too, tearing into fragments of silk and fractured words. And then it fluttered and wisped away into nothing, and her parents stood alone in the middle of the room, their hands tightly clasped. In front of them were only a few dirty shreds of pale green velvet.

Anstis was gone.

What had they done to her? Emily wanted to know, and at the same time she couldn't bear to. She looked back down at Wren instead, and wrapped the fine blankets closer around the baby. "I wish we could just go home," she whispered. "I want to go home."

Wren's black eyes glittered, and a shimmer of tiny silver lights seemed to wash over her hair. They swirled out across Emily's hand as she cradled the baby's head, and prickled lovingly over her skin.

Then the stars were all around them, glowing silver against the dark walls of the staircase. It was the same journey she and Eva had made, but the wish was taking them back so quickly that Emily was suddenly short of breath, gasping in magic instead of air.

She reached out a panicked hand to her mother, and Eva caught the very tips of her fingers. They went rushing down the starry steps together, with Ash and Gruff pounding after them.

And then they were back, and Emily had

somehow never left her chair – but it was no longer carved and ancient wood, but soft and creaking and laden with cushions. The faded old armchair in the corner of Eva's studio. They were home.

"Did you do that?" Emily whispered to the baby, who only chuckled and waved at Eva and Ash, who were standing on either side of the chair, looking shocked.

"You wished it," Gruff growled beside her. "You wanted to go home, and she brought you home by the stairs she'd seen. You did it together." Then his ears went back in surprise, as he realized he'd spoken aloud.

8

Lory had appeared at the door, with Lark and Robin behind her. She looked furious. "Where have you *been*?" she yelled at her mother. "You didn't even tell us!" Then she made an angry sort of choking noise and flung herself across the room to hug Eva. "We were worried about you," she added, her voice muffled.

"Is that the baby?" Robin asked, still standing

at the bottom of the stairs and peering up curiously.

Lory sat up straight and peered down at the blankets suspiciously. "Is it?"

"Yes." Eva showed them. "She's asleep."

"I suppose she's quite cute," Lory admitted, and Emily was certain she saw Wren wriggle, as though she'd heard.

"She's gorgeous!" Lark told her sister. "Look at all her hair!"

There was definitely an air of smugness around Wren now, and Emily giggled.

"You should rest," Ash told Eva lovingly, handing her a tiny white flower that had just appeared in his hand. "You must be exhausted."

Eva smiled at him and tucked the star of white

petals into her hair, which seemed to coil and brighten all at once. She looked a lot less tired now, Emily realized, wondering what sort of spell the glowing flower was.

"Go to bed," Ash said firmly, wrapping his arm around her waist.

Eva nodded wearily, but then she looked down at Wren and frowned. "Will you take the baby with you, Emily? There's a Moses basket in our room for her. I don't want her to be lonely – I'm not quite sure what would happen. . ."

Emily nodded. If Wren woke up and no one was watching her, who knew what she might do? Emily wouldn't put it past her to fly out of a window.

Robin fetched the Moses basket, and he and Emily settled on her bedroom window seat with

Wren in the basket on the floor beside them and Gruff sprawled over the boards next to her. Lark and Lory had stayed with Eva, curled up next to her.

"She's a bit boring," Robin said doubtfully, nudging the basket with his foot. Gruff laid back his ears, and shoved Robin with his heavy muzzle.

"Don't do that," Emily whispered crossly, reaching down to the basket and lifting their baby sister out. Wren stirred, but she didn't wake up. "She isn't boring, and you don't want to wake her."

Robin snorted, but he did reach down and very gently stroke the golden feathers that just showed above the blankets. "Especially if she tries using her wings. Mum would be a bit cross if you had to tell her you lost the baby already," he agreed, peering out of the window and looking fidgety.

"Oh, go downstairs!" Emily told him. "I'll come and find you if she wakes up, then you can meet her properly."

Robin was disappearing down the stairs practically as soon as she started talking, and Emily sighed, leaning back against her cushions and shifting the weight of the baby in her arms. The patterns in the blurred old glass of her windows were moving again, and she watched them dreamily. She hadn't been to the fairy world enough to recognize the places she saw. She probably never would be that familiar with it, she admitted to herself, a little sadly. She couldn't live in the other world, she was almost sure. Even if her parents did decide to take her, it would be too dangerous, for them as well as for Emily. But she still had her own magic, even without the beauty and excitement of a fairy world to live in. She would settle for watching it through her windows.

Smiling, Emily turned away from the glass and looked down at her little sister again. Still asleep. Emily shook her head. Robin did have a point, she supposed. Babies weren't that exciting when they were asleep. She leaned carefully over to the table in front of the window seat, wondering if she'd left a drawing pad, or a book.

There was a pad, and pencils, but on top of the pad was a parcel, which Emily most definitely hadn't left there herself. She eyed it suspiciously, wondering if it was a joke of Robin's. But it was prettily wrapped, with a ribbon, and she didn't think he would have bothered. There was a label, she noticed now, twined into the curls of ribbon, and she reached out to read it.

Hope you like this, Emily. And beside the message, a tiny drawing of a bird. A lark.

Emily started unwrapping the parcel one-handed, which was tricky. But after a couple of minutes of tugging, the ribbon simply undid itself, and lay flat on the table, and Emily realized that someone was watching her. She could feel it.

"You're awake," she murmured to Wren, whose dark eyes were fixed curiously on hers. "Did you undo the ribbon for me? Thanks."

Wren waved her arms, flapping them in a way that Emily guessed meant she wanted to be sitting up so she could see better, so Emily propped her up and pulled the paper off the parcel.

Inside was a book, one that Emily recognized. It was a recipe book that she'd bought in a charity shop, full of things to do with chocolate. But she hadn't used it much – it had turned out to be a bit old-fashioned. What had Lark done with it? Emily flicked over the pages curiously, remembering the greyish photos, and the recipe for white chocolate mice that had made white chocolate goo instead.

The recipes were not the same at all.

Lark had made her a spell book.

Wren pattered her fingers on the pages, and Emily smiled at her, and then gasped as she saw that the page changed as Wren touched it. She ran a finger down the page herself, and somehow felt the ingredients in her head. It was her spell for Brownie – the little chocolate-coloured mouse she had made Robin out of chocolate brownie crumbs. And Lark had listed the ingredients as:

Determination
Stubbornness
Jealousy
Cake
Crossness
Love
Confusion

Emily snorted. Lark was about right. Brownie had been an accident, caused by Robin assuming

Emily would never be able to do a spell. She had been so angry that he thought she was useless, she had wanted to show him. . . Gruff sniffed hungrily at the book – and Emily nodded. It smelled of chocolate, thick and sweet.

She flipped back to the title page and stroked it, and now it said *Emily's Spells. Because she can, even if she thinks she can't.*

And in very small writing underneath, *You owe me so much cake for this. Caramel toffee sponge with choccy chunks, please.*

Emily giggled, and leafed through the book, wondering which other spells Lark had described. There was a beautiful illustration of Sasha, and an account of her rescue, which said Emily was

165

brave, and a bit stupid, very loyal and probably right. It ended with, *Next time you do something that stupid, ask us to help!*

There were only about ten recipes, but even though the pages in the rest of the book were empty, Emily could tell when she stroked them that they weren't meant to stay that way. She could add her own spells to the book. She stroked the first blank page thoughtfully, and then jumped as a tiny hand landed on top of her own, the skin silken and warm.

"What are you doing?" Emily whispered to Wren, watching the glowing silver magic floating down her own fingers and pooling on the page. "Oh! The spell we used to get home. You can do this sort of thing already?" She watched, amazed, as the magic spread out and flickered into letters.

Love

Sisters

Protection

Home

Fear

Faith

The words burned themselves across the page, inscribed in the shape of an archway and then spiralling down like stairs, and Wren looked up at her, beaming, her cheeks as round as apples and pinkly shining.

"You're so clever," Emily murmured, stroking the spell and sensing the longing for home and safety that blazed out of the silvery words. She looked down at her little sister, who was still poking at the book and giggling as the letters glittered, and little stars painted themselves across the page. She was so strong. What would she be like when she was Emily's age?

"I can't wait to see," Emily murmured as Wren's fingers wrapped tightly around one of her own, and together they gazed down at the dancing magic. *I will see*, she thought to herself, turning and holding Wren up as footsteps sounded on the stairs. *I'm part of it all, I always was. And my magic will grow too.* "That's them coming back to see you," she murmured to Wren as she heard Lark shushing Robin, telling him not to wake the baby.

"She's awake already," Emily called. "It's all

right." And Wren gurgled, and clapped her plump little hands, and reached out for Robin as he curled up next to Emily on the window seat.

Emily watched him laughing as the baby patted her tiny hand against his. Wren cooed at Lark and Lory as they sent a flight of tiny birds circling around the room for her to watch. And then she leaned back against Emily, sleepy again suddenly, and pulled lovingly at Emily's dark hair that was so like her own.

Emily felt Lark wrap an arm around her shoulders, and she sighed, remembering the frightened girl who had been her mother. Had she ever held Emily in her arms, as Emily was holding Wren now, and thought about the future? For Emily it was a pathway, winding on ahead of them and leading she didn't know where. She only knew it was a place she wanted to see.

"Be happy," Emily murmured. "Wherever you are. I'm happy too."